This Is Home!

An Ivy and Mack story

Written by Rebecca Colby

Illustrated by Gustavo Mazali
with Dusan Pavlic

Collins

Who and what is in this story?

Listen and say

Download the audio at www.collins.co.uk/839829

Aunt Libby

Uncle Lee

Dad

Emma

Mum

🎧 Ivy, Mack, Mum and Dad helped Aunt Libby, Uncle Lee, Luke and Emma move to a new house.

They put things in the car. Dad took Luke's skateboard.

Mum had the radio.

SOLD

WE ARE MOVING

Ivy, Mack, Luke and Emma were in the living room. Mack helped Luke with a lamp. Ivy put some comic books in a bag.

"This is exciting!" said Ivy.

Emma was sad. "I don't want to move house. I like this house!" she said.

Ivy picked up the bag of comic books and smiled. "Home is with family, Emma."

"But *this* is home!" said Emma.

Mack laughed at Luke. The plant was too big.

"This plant is the same colour as our new sofa," said Luke.

"I liked the old sofa," said Emma.

Uncle Lee was in the kitchen. "Can you carry those boxes out to the car, please?" he asked.

Everyone picked up a box ... but not Emma.

"Mummy made my birthday cake here."

"Let's make cakes at your new house," said Mack.

"The cakes are better here," said Emma.

The children took the boxes to the cars.
"Look at me! I'm a tiger," said Mack.
"They were in a box." said Aunt Libby.
"Yes, in a box in the kitchen," said Ivy.
"They're funny," said Mum.

The children went into the garden.

"Your new garden has a tree," said Ivy.
"You can have a tree house."

"But I love THIS garden," said Emma.

Aunt Libby looked in Emma's bedroom. "Oh, let's take the bookcase to the van," she said.

"OK," said Emma.

"And panda, too!" said Ivy.

"Your new bedroom is a lot bigger," said Aunt Libby.

Emma was quiet.

"You can have sleepover parties in your new bedroom," said Ivy.

"My friends live here. Who can come?" asked Emma.

"I can come!" said Ivy.

"That's a fun idea," said Emma.

The boys were in Luke's bedroom.

Luke threw a pink school bag to Mack. "Catch, Mack!"

"That's mine!" said Emma.

14

"You can get a new bag for your *new school*," said Mack.

"You mean *OUR* school," said Ivy.

Emma smiled. "I'd like that."

Uncle Lee counted the boxes. Then he counted the people in the cars.

"Right. We need two more children."

"Goodbye, dining room. Goodbye, house."

"Don't be sad," said Ivy.

"I'm OK. There's nothing here now."

The new house was much bigger than the old house.

Emma took the key from Luke.
She opened the door to the new house.
"Come in, everyone!" she said.

The children walked in to the house.
There was a small room under the stairs.

"I can have my sleepover parties in here!"
said Emma.

Emma showed Ivy and Mack her
new bedroom. It was very big.
They laughed and danced.

"This is the best room in the house,"
said Emma.

"Isn't your new house great?" said Ivy.
Emma looked at her family.
"Yes! I love it!" she said. "THIS is home!"

Picture dictionary

Listen and repeat

bookcase

dining room

lamp

plant

sofa

stairs

1 Look and order the story

2 Listen and say

Collins

Published by Collins
An imprint of HarperCollins*Publishers*
Westerhill Road
Bishopbriggs
Glasgow
G64 2QT

HarperCollins*Publishers*
1st Floor, Watermarque Building
Ringsend Road
Dublin 4
Ireland

William Collins' dream of knowledge for all began with the publication of his first book in 1819.

A self-educated mill worker, he not only enriched millions of lives, but also founded a flourishing publishing house. Today, staying true to this spirit, Collins books are packed with inspiration, innovation and practical expertise. They place you at the centre of a world of possibility and give you exactly what you need to explore it.

© HarperCollins*Publishers* Limited 2020

10 9 8 7 6 5 4 3 2

ISBN 978-0-00-839829-3

Collins® and COBUILD® are registered trademarks of HarperCollins*Publishers* Limited

www.collins.co.uk/elt

British Library Cataloguing in Publication Data

A catalogue record for this publication is available from the British Library.

Author: Rebecca Colby
Lead Illustrator: Gustavo Mazali (Beehive)
Copy illustrator: Dusan Pavlic (Beehive)
Series editor: Rebecca Adlard
Commissioning editor: Zoë Clarke
Publishing manager: Lisa Todd
Product managers: Jennifer Hall and Caroline Green
In-house editor: Alma Puts Keren
Project manager: Emily Hooton
Editor: Deborah Friedland
Proofreaders: Natalie Murray and Michael Lamb
Cover designer: Kevin Robbins
Typesetter: 2Hoots Publishing Services Ltd
Audio produced by id audio, London
Reading guide author: Julie Penn
Production controller: Rachel Weaver
Printed and bound by: GPS Group, Slovenia

Download the audio for this book and a reading guide for parents and teachers at www.collins.co.uk/839829